85% True/
Minor Ecologies

85% true/ minor ecologies

kristen gallagher

skeleton man

ISBN-10: 0-9983715-0-5
ISBN-13: 978-0-9983715-0-4

SECOND EDITION

skeleton man
skeletonmanpress.com

Designed by Aaron Winslow & Chris Alexander.
Typeset in Stempel Garamond.

Thank you to Aaron Winslow, publisher and editor, and to Sorin Cucu, Holly Melgard, and Joshua Schuster for their generous and insightful feedback in developing this manuscript. Thanks to Ed Steck for publishing earlier versions of "Divine Remedies for Air" and "Autodidact Toad Addict" in the March 25, 2016 issue of *The Fanzine* (http://thefanzine.com/author/kristenga/), to Orchid Tierney for publishing a broadside of an earlier version of "I'm White; This is Safe for Me," and to Collective Task, curated and edited by Robert Fitterman and Klaus Killisch, for publishing an earlier version of "Archivist at Sepulcher Headquarters" (http://www.collectivetask.com/04/09/4_09_gallagher.pdf).

Thanks to the following sources, used directly in this book: "The Baffling, Gruesome Plague That Is Causing Sea Stars To Tear Themselves To Pieces," by Nathaniel Rich, May 15, 2015, *Vice.com*; "Cannibal snakes deepen Cedar Key Island mystery," April 7, 2016, *The Gainesville Herald*; *The Bay*, dir. Barry Levinson, Lionsgate 2012.

There are two Florida communities deep in the undergirding of this work, one from each coast: Kashi Ashram, my second family on the east coast; and Cedar Key, population: 98, farthest habitable island from the northeast corner of the Gulf Coast, the place where it's time to turn around.

Special thanks to Sheryl Chapman, former Secretary of the Florida Sierra Club, generous Airbnb host, and nature guide extraordinaire.

Always thanks to Chris Alexander, my favorite person. ♥

Support for this project was provided by a PSC-CUNY Award, jointly funded by The Professional Staff Congress and The City University of New York.

"85 percent of the stuff in the film is factual. I was asked at one point about doing a documentary about the Chesapeake Bay, which is 40 percent dead. I looked into it, gathered the facts, and thought, it's pretty scary. ... Then I realized we've gathered all this research; why don't we tweak it for a theatrical release? We can scare an audience with a story that is 80 to 85 percent science and facts."
—Barry Levinson, Director, *The Bay*

"They go down in the phosphate mines and bring up the wet dust of the bones of pre-historic monsters, to make rich land in far places, so that people can eat. But, all of it is not dust. Huge ribs, twenty feet from belly to backbone. Some old-time sea monster caught in the shallows on that morning when God said, 'Let's make some more dry land. Stay there, great Leviathan! Stay there as a memory and a monument to Time.' Shark teeth as wide as the hands of a working man. Joints of a backbone three feet high, bearing witness to the mighty monster of the deep when the Painted Land rose up and did her first dance with the morning sun. Gazing on these relics, forty thousand years old and more, one visualizes the great surrender to chance and change when these creatures were rocked to sleep and slumber by the birth of the land."
—Zora Neale Hurston, *Dust Tracks on a Road*

"And with these, the sense of the world's concreteness, irreducible, immediate, tangible, of something clear and closer to us: of the world, no longer as a journey having constantly to be remade, not as a race without end, a challenge having constantly to be met, not as the one pretext for a despairing acquisitiveness, nor as the illusion of a conquest, but as the rediscovery of a meaning, the perceiving that the earth is a form of writing, a geography of which we had forgotten that we ourselves are the authors."
—Georges Perec, *Species of Spaces*

Cloud Iridescence

I have imagined a great drying up, a water crisis, everything catching fire. I've pictured total flooding, an apocalyptic winter, snow covering New York City for millennia. But I never imagined our material experience of light suddenly changing. Why do we treat light as if it were transparent? It's not. We just evolved, eyes are entrenched responses to what has been there "to see," "clear" means matching the demands of the occasion, "empty" is only things we can't perceive. What if an increase in heat melted all the reflective surfaces in our atmosphere into new angles, and light finally appeared.

We were out fishing. The day began calm, glass like, sky and water in the usual reflective diptych, our boat the only disturbance in the blue globe, soft ripples disappearing into lumps of quicksand. Ahead, the moving edge of the horizon, a fold in the blue.

In the upper right edge of my peripheral vision, a weird vibration in the sky. We hesitate. Time either stops or passes. I turn and see Jaya Priya turning toward me, but we snap to look up again, a weird rainbow pulsing in the sky. Does it move when I move? I rock back and forth to see. Am I having a stroke, a brain episode, my eyes, it's starting, but I feel fine. The vibration of the rainbow moves with my eyes, my eyes seem to be making rainbows out of light. I close my eyes, reverse my gaze backward along my optic nerves, to where they plug into my forebrain, relax, then look out again. It's still there. A rainbow coming from a cloud, a blurry rainbow encircling a cloud like the rings of Saturn. I say guys do you see that and someone else is already saying whoa before I finish. Ok it's real. We google it. Sunlight is melting ice in the clouds at our latitude.

Disaster-by-Numbers

I use accuweather.com because I find it more accurate than other weather sites. They have a feature called "Minute Cast." To get to it, you go to the hourly forecast page, then you click the Minute Cast button, and from the Minute Cast page you can scroll down and click "Radar" for the radar visualization of the weather where you are.

It's been raining in Okeechobee. Big red blobs keep forming over the word Okeechobee on the map, which means the rain is drenching and blinding over the north half of the lake, where a hurricane in 1928 killed 2,500 people, mostly African Americans, which also happens at the end of *Their Eyes Were Watching God* by Zora Neale Hurston, who draws from first-hand accounts of the storm. The hurricane burial ground sprawls for miles. That's where it's raining now.

My apocalyptic future fantasy has come to be all about floods. The world flooded, all water, a few survivors living on a series of boats tied together by rope. A flotilla-city. I've been reading about it and I ask you, how are these visions not already true? How is this not a documentary about the weather? Because it's the future weather? Because we know it's going to happen? It's already happening in our minds.

Some days I think the only thing real is the coming flood, that all the other stories are just distractions from that fact. So I'm not concerned with making fun of the guy in Florida who thought he could steal a chainsaw from Walmart by stuffing it in his pants and then, yes, of course, sawed off his own leg in the store, and it ended up in the newspaper, then on the twitter feed of "Florida Man," and then in some Dave Barry book. I'm not interested in any of that except for its relationship to how distracted we are from the coming flood, the red blob over Okeechobee that may soon be the red blob over everything, which would be the Fulfillment of My Fantasy, and you know what Lacan says about that—you die when that happens.

Out over the Oyster Tomb

Here where the Suwannee meets the Gulf are the first signs of a human garbage collection and memorial system. The people lived on oysters and clams and discarded the shells into one huge pile. The pile extended variously, grew veins, and people placed mementos and detritus between the shells. No one knows when or how the practice emerged because it's been dated back to before western recorded time.

The detritus provided extra support for the shells in the mound, but archeologists have also determined that some of what was placed there has qualities of memorializing, or the disposal of prized objects—a swatch of decorated fabric, a carved handle of a knife. There's also seemingly insignificant detritus, though significance could be personal to the placer and not interpretable by science.

Mounds formed indefinitely, were ongoing and multi-directional, with no clear end, like mourning, like time. If the mound's relationship to the dead is primary, if it was a place of memorializing or mourning, it's not hard to imagine the area of the mounds as a place to commune with the dead.

It feels heavy to be there. The gravity is stronger, the pitch in the sound of the air lower. There are no ready explanations here, only evidence that a trash pile or a funeral pile or a memory pile or a kind of haunted calendar exists.

A leader of the Creek Indian Nation came to speak there and jokingly said the message of the mound is to remain taller than the grave and lower than the sky; that's why they made paths to walk to the tops of the mound—the higher you go, the more death is there, and if you go too high, if you go too far up, you could fall off the edge of the earth.

Tales from Cannibal Snake Island

The Black Dog Bar in Cedar Key, where I tend bar, has one of the best beer selections in Florida, certainly the single best beer selection from Spring Hill to Apalachicola, and a generous, rustic, wrap-around porch hanging over the swampy edge of the northeastern Gulf, surrounded by wild oysters.

Most weekdays, anytime from around 3 to 5 pm, scientists and grad students from the University of Florida come in. They run experiments out in the islands near here. The Black Dog isn't the closest bar to where they dock, but it's where folks with curiosity come, people willing to try something besides Bud or Miller.

One day they come in early. First it's Cohle and his new grad students. I don't know Cohle well, but I observe him, half his head shaved and the other half long and, being in this part of Florida, that's interesting. And he's not afraid to drink interesting beer. But he's shy, plays it close, uses few words. But today is different somehow. His eyes are darting around as he orders his IPA, he looks confused, distracted, upset.

Yesterday, they were drinking and playing corn-hole — the bar is big enough inside we can have a cornhole game in the middle — and they just seemed like dorks getting to know each other. Today, they arrive early and seem off-kilter, wide-eyed, impressed, pacing, staggering a little, foreheads wrinkled. Two senior scientists dash through directly to the porch without ordering beers.

Serious conversations and sudden outbursts, people talking on their phones more than usual. Finally Cohle comes to refresh his beer. I ask what's up.

"You know Seahorse, right over here?"

"Yeah, sure," I nod, "All the birds."

"Not anymore." Takes a glug of beer.

"What do you mean?"

"Birds vanished."

"What do you mean?" Still not understanding.

"I mean that yesterday there were birds, today no birds."

There's no one else in the bar so I follow him to the porch. From what I overhear, the team arrived before sunrise to an eerie quiet, a silence beyond silence, an echoing lack of anything being present, absolute stillness, the sound of the sudden vanishing of the life force of 20,000 birds sleeping in their nests. And at sunrise, where there's usually chirping and fluttering, still nothing. We watch a smartphone video of all the cracked eggs on the ground:

Abandoned nests

Birds do not abandon nests unless a traumatic event occurs

And this many species, all at once
In the middle of the night
There is a one-in-five-million chance
We have thousands
Literally tens of thousands
And only three dead birds
You can pick up a cracked egg and see the
developing bird fetus inside
It reminds me of a show, do you know it, the main
characters get put in some kind of cocoon trapped
under a thin membrane in like a cave or a basement.
Was that Star Trek?
Yeah maybe
This is a pelican egg
It looks like a miniature pterodactyl sleeping
This is the chickadee egg
Aww, just a small blob!
Theories are bandied about—rare diseases, invasive
species, human vandals, a drone—but no consensus
emerges. They have three bird carcasses to test for disease
or signs of predation. They've sent them back to the lab.
One of the scientists keeps talking about synchronicity,
"there's never been such synchronicity—so many species
doing the same thing at once!" He was going to write a
paper about that.

   A vandal, any person would need a hatchet and a lot
   of time to set up camp there

Yeah, no way, there's no evidence
No way
By the end of the day, we know more.
It turns out those three dead birds just got pummeled
on the way out
From their autopsies?
We learned it wasn't any of the possible things
So now it's the impossible things
Things look different now
Must have been a tough evacuation
That's 20,000 birds
Some of them not so little
Plus, the trees
And only three died
Yeah that's damn good flying
Amazing
One of the regulars—Phil, an ex-Marine who still listens to his military radio and probably has a whole illegal subaltern radio universe set up at his house—says that around the time of the incident there was a spike in people calling to complain about low-flying planes and helicopters at night.
So, what, the birds are all in their nests and suddenly there's a helicopter?
A helicopter with a floodlight dropping in?
As of now, Phil's is the only theory left standing, corroborated when Bobby, the owner and my boss, brings in a copy

of *The Gainesville Herald* with an article saying there's an investigation linking the bird disappearance to a statement from the US Navy alerting all US citizens of secret, unannounced military exercises in biologically sensitive areas, including Wildlife Sanctuaries and breeding habitats.

Postscript—

A month later, Cohle comes in alone, looking a bit shaken. Instead of going straight out to the porch, he sits right in front of me, by the red velvet lamp with the dangling yellow crystals. After he downs the 10% ABV from France, he says, "Snakes're desperate. It's a rough world out there."

He describes a snake lunging at him at his first step onto land this morning: "My right foot was still in the boat. I could see they are all way skinnier than they should be. Lots of signs of aggression, moving more, and faster than normal. I jumped and it missed me, it barely missed me, and landed in the water."

I learn through this that in fact, Cohle is the snake guy, he studies the snakes, and there's a special situation with the snakes on Seahorse. Before the disappearance, the snakes had gourmet meals falling from the sky, fresh fish bits falling from birds' mouths, whole fish accidentally dropping from nests, gourmand birds vomiting up fish paté. These snakes exhibited different and fewer patterns of aggression; they never had to kill to eat.

He says he got out of there, fast, but as he was pulling away he saw a cottonmouth eat another cottonmouth, which means all the other food on the island is gone — raccoons, clams and oysters, worms, anole, shrimp, crab, barnacle — gone, all gone. He gets an IPA, tells me a little about himself, what music he likes, then just gets drunker and drunker. His final efforts of the night involve showing me video results from searching "snake eating other snake" and "snake cannibal." He eventually falls asleep in one of the antique dentist chairs on the far side of the cornhole court. We let him sleep. Bobby agrees to stay and play video games on the couch until he wakes up.

Autodidact Toad Addict

The toads began as part of an experiment by US agents working in Colombia to breed a range of amphibians for special skills in pest control in industrial farming. As soon as Toad 6140E-1 Buford Marinus demonstrated the triple threat of strength, predation, and toxicity, the exotic animals black market had a suitcase full of their eggs on a plane to Miami, with a guy who later admitted that he was supposed to hand off the suitcase to a contact at the airport. But when he left the container full of toad eggs at the dropoff point, someone reported the unaccompanied package to authorities, who determined its contents, and treated the eggs as a potential biohazard. We now know that sometime during transport the eggs hatched and a group of Buford Marinus got loose in the wildlife refuge adjacent to the airport.

Rumors have spread that US Sugar sponsored the research and paid to smuggle in the illegal toad eggs, that US Sugar will do anything to stop their problem with white grubs eating their sugar cane. Whatever the cause, the toads have taken over South Florida.

These supertoads can leap up to twelve feet and, in addition to white grubs, they eat native frogs and toads, any fish or bird under six inches long, kittens and puppies, but prefer, above all, canned pet food, and will fight pets for it. They will also eat dead or rotten matter, if hungry enough.

Buford Marinus also shoots a highly toxic milky substance from the large parotoid glands behind its ears, covering its own body and everything for three feet around, creating a Buford Toxin puddle the color of almond milk. There are stories of them leaping from trees, latching onto a person's thigh or a dog's rear, and emitting the toxin onto what they grab, leaving a scar. There are stories of kids throwing these toads at their enemies, hoping to do them harm.

Buford Toxin both immobilizes and burns whatever it comes into contact with. Other symptoms of Buford Toad Contact Poisoning include drooling, head-shaking, crying, loss of coordination, burn mark at the location where the toad grabbed you or was thrown into you, and a burning sensation in that same area.

In addition to releasing toxins and jumping twelve feet, Buford Marinus makes impressive exits by inflating its lungs, puffing up, and lifting its body off the ground, up and away like a balloon or tiny toy helicopter. Some toads are said to hold their breath for up to four minutes, and the longer they hold their breath, the faster they accelerate upward, like in a dream. When they run out of breath, they deflate and drop to earth wherever they land, but they are so meaty and strong that this happens with just a hefty bounce, no injury.

But, reader, let me tell you, while you may be scared that weaponized, poisonous toads will soon be falling from the sky in a town near you, think again. They are more likely to enter from below. Most home sewer systems are "open," meaning that at some point between every house and the main sewer line, or in the sewer line itself, a pipe has separated or broken, so anything can get in. Toads now nest in and travel throughout area sewer systems, and are primarily making their invasions into human homes through toilets.

This happened to someone I know. Her aunt poured a bleach solution into the toilet and left it to do its work. A few minutes later, she heard her dog barking furiously, and splashing noises coming from the bathroom. When she went in, a giant frog was sitting and staring at her from the toilet bowl. She went to grab it but it leapt at her and grabbed her face. She could feel the liquid burning as it ran down her cheek and neck, but she assumed it was the bleach. But then she started to lose feeling in her face. The frog went limp and fell off, landing in the pool of water at the base of her plug-in waterfall sculpture, which she keeps in the hallway by the entrance to the bathroom. She cares about animals, she was hoping to wash the bleach off and save it, but the animal died. Then the aunt collapsed and became temporarily paralyzed from the toxin. Now there's a burn scar on her face with a frog shape to it, its arm now permanently reaching around her face to grab her nose.

Weird facts and rumors continue to emerge: militiamen in Geneva milking supertoad toxin and using it as an arrow poison; toads meaty enough to feed a family of four (after the careful removal of the poisonous skin and parotoid glands); the meat is an excellent source of omega-3 fatty acids; the toxin in small doses is both an aphrodisiac and a hair restorer; the Disaster Zones applied for a contract to use it in pregnancy testing, a mandated, monthly, enforced, but well-paid job there, which for some proves the government has always been behind the underground bufo toxin market.

What matters to me the most is that in powdered form, mixed with raw cacao for taste, a small amount of supertoad toxin will get you high enough to sleep through the night. There's a solid black market for it in the Disaster Zones, where powdered supertoad toxin is the new oxycontin.

Homeowners, Forest Rangers, and pest control experts alike have obsessed over methods for trapping, killing, and deterring the frogs. Town meetings have been held and study groups formed to try to eliminate this invasive species. But experts agree it's most likely too little, too late.

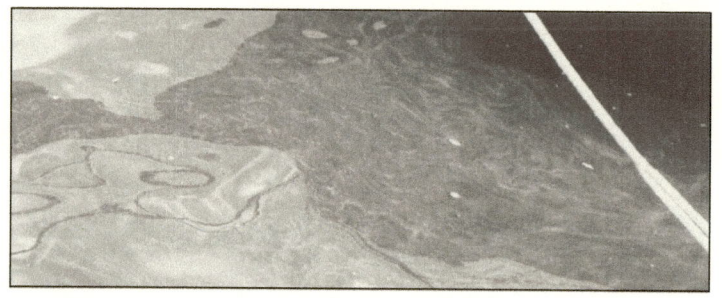

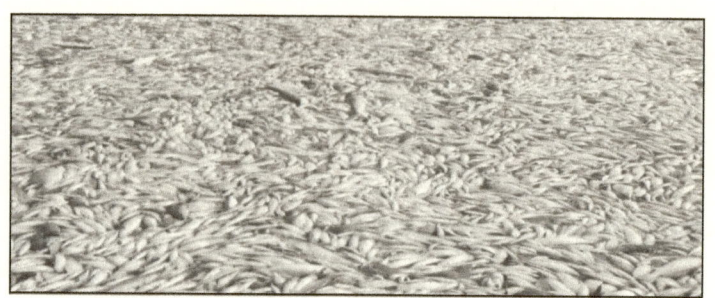

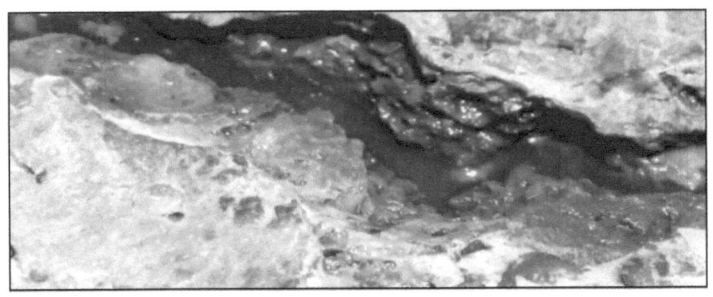

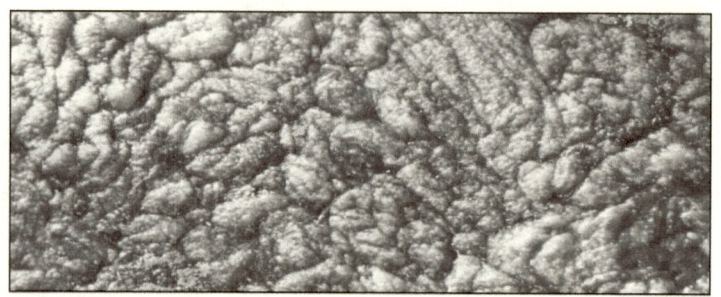

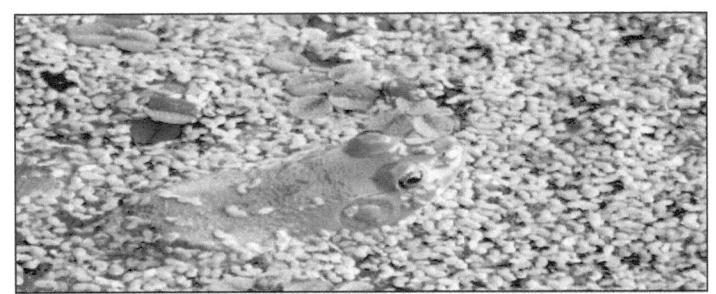

Death To Our Friends

Mison Gora knows sea stars have no blood, brain, or central nervous system; they do not form emotional attachments. Still, having spent most of her life observing them, she has formed a deep attachment to the stars. She built her modest clay home in Indian River County, Florida because stars were known to gather in its tidal pools. Her home looks out onto a series of such pools. I chose her airbnb partly for this view and partly because of her work with the stars. And because of my interest in her work, she let me into her world.

All her life she was fascinated by the stars. She saw them first in tanks as a child in the Midwest, where her father's chemistry lab sat proximate to a research aquarium. She would go after school and spend hours sitting quietly, staring into the tanks.

"I became fascinated by how many ocean creatures are not fish," she told me, "and rarely move. They sit, breathing water."

Her bookshelves contain every mention of sea stars in history, an exhaustive collection. Every night she would talk me through her library. Ancient books like *The Creation Song*, an ancient prayer to the gods who made the stars take form on earth, and Georg Eberhard Rumpf's 1705 *The Ambonese Curiosity Cabinet*, where he reports that sea stars can feel thunderstorms approaching, and one can predict hurricanes by observing them "grab hold of earth with their little legs, looking to...hold themselves down as if with anchors."

Mison is part of a small global community who still believe the stars predict things related to weather and the ecosystem, including the fate of the earth. She has a photo of herself with Sri Sai Kaleshwar Swami and a signed copy of his 2002 book *The Divine Mystery Fort*, where he asserts "as the stars go, so goes the universe." She read her favorite part to me: "Sometimes at the full moon time, when the moon is really dazzling and hitting on the ocean, a starfish jumps out of the water and falls down. If you can get that star, you can suck unbelievable cosmic energy from it. You can use it as your own power object."

"Have you tried that?" I ask.

"I have."

She says it's been a mostly peaceful life here off the central east coast of Florida, not very touristy, quiet, surrounded by diverse landscapes that produce interesting microclimates. But she told me one disturbing story from

Memorial Day weekend 2013. On that Saturday, she woke and found the bat stars, normally active scavengers, all glommed together in one single ball, perfectly still. They reproduce asexually, so this wasn't a mating ritual. She peeled them apart, one by one, which they resisted. It took about 30 minutes. Then she found what they had been consuming: the corpse of an ochre star, their neighbor for the past five years.

Two days later she noticed that some of the other stars did not look well. Their arms were twisted around their stomachs like they were trying to hug themselves, their texture looked thin and mushy, "like fading party balloons." By the next day one of the stars had lost an arm. But the day after that, she said, was horrible.

"The rocks looked like an asteroid battlefield," she wrinkled up her nose in squeamish disgust. The stars had become squishy and pockmarked with white lesions, their pink and white guts spilling out, oozing all over the rocks, fleshy, more arms detached, and the arms continued to crawl, disembodied, along the rocks.

She knew sea stars shed their arms in times of stress. She said it is not uncommon to see from her window a curious child pick up a star by one of its limbs, and then the child jumps back, shudders or screams, and begins calling for its mother. "The star jettisons that arm to escape," Mison laughs, smiles wide, a glint in her eye, "Imagine if someone grabbed your arm and you didn't like it, you just let that arm fly off. No problem, I'll re-generate a new arm later."

But this time was different. These stars were using one arm to rip off the other. She watched for hours and hours, days and nights. "They twisted their arms together and pulled and pulled and pulled until one of the arms popped off, then that arm just walks away, like it doesn't even know it's dead." This continued for about a week, nearly every species of star ripping off its arms, one after the other. She'd have coffee watching them rip off one or two arms, then she'd go make lunch, and by the time she came back each one had ripped off two more. In the final days, the leather star and the last of the ochres liquefied.

The bat stars were the only ones left alive. For them, the mass death of their friends was a bonanza. They gorged on the corpses.

Divine Remedies for Air

There is a legend that on his mission to find La Florida and the Fountain of Youth, Ponce de Leon had been charged with carrying a gift representing his sponsor, Ferdinand II of Aragon. De Leon was instructed to trade this statue with whoever was "the truest leader," the one who held The Fountain of Youth. But the legendary part is this: this statue, "Il Christo Degli Abissi," Christ of the Abyss, was lost just beyond what is now Key West, in a battle with pirates. De Leon himself says he watched his charge crash through the surface of the sea, then sink into a tiny crevice at the bottom of the shallow ocean there.

Divers and Treasure Hunters have searched for it since. Was it taken by the current and coughed up into the Gulf? No, the trawlers and oil riggers would have found it by now. Was it taken on toward Havana, or maybe further? No, it likely would have been too heavy to get far in the light currents of the archipelago's shallow waters. I like to think that it fell into a crevice and came out the other side, and now it's in some Mongolian grandma's shrine. But everyone agrees it must be here, so cave divers continue to come.

There's also a fake version off Key Largo. A guy put a concrete statue of Christ underwater in a shallow area along the way to a popular reef, and if you pay him, he'll tell you the story and take you to the statue. There's no underwater cave. You just snorkel to a statue of Jesus in a three foot deep tidal pool.

Divers of every stripe, with every motive, from every part of the world come to the area to try to find the real one, the mythic one, so much so that some people now call that part of the ocean "The Christ Abyss." No one has ever found the statue and many who try never return.

Cave divers die often, they disappear and everyone assumes they just got caught in a tight spot and ran out of oxygen, or went too deep and fried their brains, or miscalculated and took a wrong turn—imagine a darkness so dark you can't see your hand right in front of your face, the eyes strain to find something, anything, to see, and fail utterly—lines snap or become entangled, clips and fittings jam, regulators and dump valves malfunction, light sources fail, people get cocky with their breathing gas management.

In 1969 a group of misfit intellectuals and spiritualists from Ohio moved to Fleming Key based on a call felt by their leader, a man they alternately called "father," "guru," and "Nick." Guru Nick was a painter who had studied in the Himalayas and who led groups on epic quests to find places like Shambhalla and Shangri-la and who had a dream he held his breath to infinity and dove down into a sea that seemed endlessly deep, until he found a statue of Christ, tattered and barnacled but arms still outstretched, head tilted, welcoming, with a placard at the base that read:

"Videmis nunc per speculum in aenigmate"

"In an enigma by means of a mirror"

A line from St. Paul.

And nearby, two human skulls, one blacker and more smoothed over with age.

Guru Nick and his followers more than searched for the statue; they came to define their work in near-religious terms. They wrote epic poems honoring every character in the story and every diver who never returned; they created a series of prayers, toasts, and rituals around the history. They equated their search with the human search for meaning in the universe. Today, the last of Guru Nick's followers is eighty and has given up diving due to physical limitations associated with old age. But she is the keeper and caretaker of all the rituals and prayers, and educates others in the ways of the Christ Abyss.

In earlier, distant times, this was a town of escapees, people who dropped out of a life elsewhere, a kind of metaphorical "end of the line." When it came to the Christ Abyss, townspeople heard the story, but many wondered, "what is there in a cave worth dying for." But today, as a result of Nick and his followers, the town has come to know itself as a place central to the Christ Abyss legend, and the town culture operates around one optimistic idea: maybe the statue really is there. That possibility has become the mythos through which the community defines itself, immersed in the activities of the sea, perceiving itself through the mirror of a lost underworld.

Each night at half-past sunset, the hour by which all divers should return, in all the tiki bars across town, locals raise a glass to mourn those who came to die here. For the toast, it is customary to recite any of the following lines: "they lived according to a sublime astronomy," "the caves are outer space inside the earth," and, "if we can see the Abyss, like we can see the Milky Way, it's because it exists somewhere inside us" and everyone clinks glasses.

The Codes for Extinction

The Florida Scrub Jay is not going to make it.

The endemic bird relies on territory for survival, a very specific scrub habitat, and that territory is, more and more, becoming prime real estate. I had heard scrub jays were friendly. Diane Ackerman, in *The New Yorker*, said they were garrulous, trusting, friendly. So I took a Greyhound to Clewiston and paid an ambulance driver to take me two hours north toward Venus, to the southern end of the Lake Wales Ridge. The Ridge is a strip of sand running up the center of the state of Florida. It's special because that sand has never been submerged in water. It's from Pangea and used to be connected to the Sahara. While only two hundred feet above sea level, in a state notorious for its flatness, this two hundred feet demonstrates how such a small difference in elevation creates a significantly different ecosystem. This strip is the closest thing Florida has to "mountains," but these mounds are actually, as the scientists say, "ancient islands."

On the ride north, we pass a sign for Immokalee, famous for the hunger strike and other actions of migrant tomato pickers who successfully moved against their bosses and Taco Bell, the major buyer of Immokalee tomatoes. They struggled hard to expose their situation and won their fight for higher pay and better working conditions. My friend helped design their website.

But we turn right, towards the fields of endless sugar cane. These are the parts of Florida frequented by mostly Big Farm bosses, migrant workers, and real estate developers trying to buy land from US Sugar. But of course there's also a Walmart, and the Walmart has a small pizza shop next to it, which we stop at, and it turns out the owners are from Philly. The pizza is good, for Florida.

Archbold Biological Station is a giant preserve and study area paid for by an environmentalist family descended from a man named Archbold. They've built an educational slice of heaven around a weird little ecosystem. A slice of the Sahara in Florida is transporting, time of the white sands, oceanic Gaia in the sky. No one lives here except hundreds of endemic species, the ten or twenty scientists who study them, and their staff. I have never felt so remote.

When I arrive, I roll down the car window to ask the first person I see, a young woman, directions for where to check in. Within an hour, I see her again. Her visiting scientist dorm room is next to my visiting writer dorm room. She invites me for a beer on the patio. She is a graduate student earning credit for taking part in the scrub jay census. She invites me out the next day with her and her thesis director to take part in the census. We finish our beers and watch the Sahara sunset. By sunrise we are waist high in the scrub.

Each scrub jay has been tagged, the impossibly tiny color-coded identification bracelets piled up on the impossibly tiny legs of each one. My task is, with binoculars, to see, read, and check off boxes identifying these bracelets. A scrub jay leg is about half an inch long, and many of them have two or three bracelets on. The lead scientists and the grad student know the birds well; they quickly check each bracelet off a list full of associated codes. They know which bird is which code, and they know where the codes are on the giant grids of codes they carry. I can't see shit.

But I do see evolution, how a thing obtains to its environment. Like a tiny, dirty, matted, blue bird skidding sideways into a sandy path, pecking around searching for the peanut I threw out to bring it here so I could read its tagged leg. It has learned my presence means peanuts. Like the way this scrub habitat needs lightning and wildfires to keep it short and scrubby – conditions necessary for the survival of scrub jays. But real estate doesn't like lightning and fire. These jays are blocking real estate. We are studying their extinction.

The head scientist refers to *The New Yorker* article, asks if I've read it, says he didn't like it, she made the scrub jays cute. He calls the scrub jays "kind of a stupid sucker species," "snacks for hawks sitting in a bowl of exposure," and describes to me how they swarm and peck the brains out of their enemy mockingbirds, peck out the mockingbird's brain through its eyes, "which is what the real nature writing would tell you," he says, but concedes that Ackerman "probably felt the need to market the scrub jay, and *The New Yorker* would most likely prefer the story of a friendly sweet bird going extinct, because it's sad and people will feel moved and more actively involved with nature by reading that, and it is sad, but we shouldn't need that in order to care, and they aren't nice, they are stupid and mean unless you have Planters peanuts on you.

"If you stand back, it's just another moment in a territory, another vector of earth's story through one bird, and yes, of course it's human activity that's forcing them to die off, and their extinction will set off a chain of other losses, we all know that, now it's just a matter of watching it happen and trying to learn everything we can from it." He throws a handful of peanuts in every direction and casts a wide gaze just above the horizon.

Scrawny, filthy, matted, spastic little blue and gray bird, come closer, yes, I have the peanut.

"Dash azure silver is routinely with cops," he tells me, as if I know the birds' code names, and then a swarm of jays arrive, flocking, darting, landing, skidding, pecking, taking off again.

He recognizes each one, recites the codes as he checks them off:

Q dash.

No, QN dash B.

We did not have white lime last time.

QR dash A.

Q dash hot orange is male from NWTR.

Q red dash flesh silver flesh.

Green white clover dash hot.

Clover dash lime white.

Clover dash lime green.

Lime hot clover dash.

He intersperses his code reading with chat.

Have you read this guy something-shames, writes about Key West and about New Yorkers in Florida?

No, I haven't!

Have you seen David Attenborough's *Life of Birds*?

No, I haven't! Is that sheep?

No, it's an eastern narrowmouth toad which isn't a true toad. To study frog calls you have to stay up all night. I'm a morning person.

That bullfrog sounds like a hand bike pump.

Have you read *Beast in the Garden*, about big cats coming into Colorado?

No, I haven't!

Have you read *The Tiger*, about a Russian pacific coast tiger who ate 2 people?

No, I haven't!

Have you seen *The Ghost Into Darkness*—

about these lion brothers who killed, like, many many people, because they were encroaching on their territory?
Silver dash lime green hot.
Hot pink clover dash silver flesh silver.
QR dash Z.
What's he doing over here?
Q dash hot pink.
Q dash flesh gold blue.
That's really strange what are they doing here?
Clover dash lime white.
Green white clover dash hot.

We finish by noon and only four birds—two parents and two offspring—are unaccounted for. He suspects they've been ousted by other scrub jays for territory, says they were "not much for fighting." We get back in the truck and go to the cafeteria for lunch.

I'm White; This is Safe for Me

The South Florida Crackers live in isolated communities, on boats conjoined by rope, some have docks and small homes, some have small sheds on land to keep stuff. Out on the water and in hidden coves they live, eat, drink, sell marijuana, marijuana gummies and vodka gummies and eat the fish they catch. On offer: blackened mullet, jambalaya of shrimp or sand fleas, grilled mahi or bass on a good day, and everyone has a case of cheap watery beer or makes punch out of leftover punches, and no one speaks of race, because everyone here is white, and just wants to have a good time, I am told.

One guy I really liked named Rudy,
who was missing a front tooth and
who was super charming and cute
who told me the missing tooth was from one of his many boat accidents
who wants to move to the Cayman Islands
who wishes to no longer pay taxes

who knows who Zora Neale Hurston is
who didn't even flinch when I said I was there for Zora
Neale Hurston
who just seemed happy and impressed and gave advice
about a museum I should go to
who knew about the art history there
which is the art history of Fort Pierce
which is the nearest town
the town I am in
the town where Zora died
the town where Zora was buried and was buried without
a headstone
until Alice Walker came and found the unmarked grave
until Alice Walker raised money and got her a headstone
and Rudy knows about that
and Rudy knows the art that is there
and he tells me of the big group of artists that all hung out
and drank and had sex with each other and made art
and Rudy is impressed by that
so he takes me out on his boat and everyone says be careful
as we are leaving be careful be careful
and I hold my cheap can of beer and prepare myself
for death.
We find a dark cove and snorkel.
The reef has eyes inside of it that look out at night, there's
something in there.

Archivist at Sepulcher Headquarters

DOSSIER
CONCERNING: ARGULUS
DATE FOUND: June 21, 3032
DATE(S) of artifact(s): Various, 2011-2020
Location found: S. Atl.
Lat. 27° 43.7'N Long. 80° 22.65'W
Caught in Nuestra Regala

Description:

red metal capsule, 12" H x 8" W x 8" D
6 artifacts, various dates, arranged from most recent

Artifact 1

Tape of recording marked "WKSO-TV"
"Independence Day, 2020"

Description:

Moving images:
debris on the front lawns and the streets
dead fish washing ashore at the inlet
reams of dead fish rolling in with the tide
scientist says, "we are looking"
off-camera voice says, "look to your left"
and
"it's a beautiful day"
teenage girls' feet dangling over pool water
kids playing in the sprinkler
a mouth biting a slice of watermelon
a blue crab walking sideways underwater

An interview:
"I'm here with this year's Miss Crustacean, Miss Sally White,
Sally how do you feel about being Miss Crustacean?"
"It's every girl's dream to be Miss Crustacean"

Cut to image:
people fishing off the back of a motorboat

Cut to:
two dead bodies found in the inlet with strange bites
recorded quotes laid over:
"not shark, not jellyfish, not manowar, not snake"
"oceanographers from the university are looking"
"we think it's feeding off the nutrients in the water from
the runoff"
"the mayor says talk to the EPA"
"the governor has all but defunded us"
"and hasn't been returning our calls"
"it is killing everything"
"mercury levels way up"
"OCBs, PCBs, endocrine suckers, viagra, estrogen, giar-
dia, and trace amounts of pretty much you name it"

Cut to:
young white male dressed in all black, in front of a fence
"one of these chicken sheds has 32,000 chickens in it, they
eat about 10,000 pounds worth of food, which leads to 45
million pounds of chicken shit dumped into nearby rivers
and streams each year, and that shit has the hormones and
steroids fed to the chickens for their breast growth"
YWM climbs the fence
"from here, the chicken waste runoff"

"and the desalination plant converts it to drinking water"
"and in fact it increases the amount of chickens that can
be grown"

Cut to:
middle aged white man speaking at podium
"we grew up in the water, we swim in the water, we fish in
the water"
"our lawns benefit from that, we have pools full of it, and
it's the best darn water anywhere"
he drinks a glass of it
a hesitant, labored gulp.

Cut to:
A woman in a white lab coat points to a radar screen
"the toxins are moving north"
cut to Miss Crustacean in a bathing suit in the dunking booth
cut to Miss Crustacean dunked
cut to Miss Crustacean recording video of herself breaking
out in a weird rash
cut to 8 people vomiting blood after a crab eating contest

Cut to:
"Mark, I'm being told doctors checked to see if it was
EBOLA, but it wasn't, and now the CDC is being
brought in. Also, the health department has issued a
warning suggesting children, elders, and people with

compromised immune systems spend minimal time in the water."

Cut to:
young woman with the same rash as Miss Crustacean, speaking into her iPhone camera
"my name is LaMia Jezcik, and I'm in the Emergency Room of Sebastian General Hospital"
she shows us her flesh rotting off her shoulder

[End]

_____

Artifact 2

Personal Diary / Log of Captain Mike Delpech. Treasure Coast Fleet #111, Florida
Date: August, 2036

Argulus, now King of the Sea Bacteria, I knew he'd come for us, that dome-shelled, beady-eyed vampire of the sea. Now his antennae have modified into barbed suckers, his scraping mouthparts can dig through flesh, and the enzyme he secretes turns digestive tissue into drinkable sludge.

I know argulus better than any human. I have spent my life observing its habits. I was the first to notice them growing larger and more aggressive. I am the one who in the early aughts tried to demonstrate the potential problem with this by arranging a little show for the local officials.

Down by the center of town, just off the central tourism area, approaching the docks, I put a fresh pig carcass in a cage and placed it in a pool of our drinking water. I used a glass pool so people could see inside. Spent half my retirement on renting the pool. To the current drinking water I added water I infused with higher amounts of the hormones and drugs already found, and on the increase, in our drinking water. Then I added a bucket of water full of argulus I had been letting grow in this drug-mixture. The drug-fed argulus had grown enough so that they were still barely visible in water, but when they moved together they formed a faint grey cloud. When I dumped them into the pool they entered the pigs' orifices in dark droves. They prefer to feast from the inside out.

Every day I dumped some shrimp in the pool. The argulus took shifts congregating on the cage bars to prevent the other arthropods from getting a bite. When shrimp approached, the argulus devoured them in minutes. By the end of the fourth day, the pig was reduced to a pile of bones.

But people refused to see the implications. They called me a stuntman. But the argulus continued to grow in size, numbers, and ferocity. Now they believe. Some say it was the sludge from the chicken plant, some say it was a combination of chemical dumping, super-fertilizer runoff, and bacterial growth from algae in the water. I know longer ask why.

When I was kid we lived on a boat and I swam every day. I would go down and look to see how many crabs our cages had caught for dinner. I used to climb out of the water, up the ladder, with a crab in each hand, and little sea lice would drop off them and bite the webbing between my toes. Those were very different times.

———————————

Artifact 3

Newspaper clipping, *Broward County Herald*
Date: September 10, 2013

Finding a dead body in the ocean may sound gruesome, but for forensic scientists it is simply perplexing. Although the way a body decomposes on land is well understood, much less is known about how human remains fare underwater.

"We have had a lot of disarticulated feet wash up on our shores in running shoes lately," says Anderson. "We think this may show how crab and shrimp activity can result in severed limbs."

Artifact 4

Transcript of voice recording
Marked: "July 13, 2027 "

[unclear voice for first 0:05:13]

"Oceanographers have found an increase in infected fish. Inside the fishes mouths they're finding small lice-like creatures sucking the blood out of the fishes innards, but the fish are still alive. They think the eggs are swallowed by fish and then they hatch inside the fish's belly, and start eating it away, eventually taking the place of the digestive system itself, it's fun stuff, but I've never seen a parasite like this, and so many, I reported it to the environmental council and they're looking into it."

[recording deteriorates, cannot hear for 0:20:33]

"...the lice have grown to several centimeters thick and are so numerous they cover the entire shoreline. they've been able to fight off all other arthropods, even the Giant Three Spot Shrimp. In just a few days there was nothing left but sand, water, and a black cloud floating close to the water's edge. Then the giant lice lost interest and left. After a few days several much larger lice crawled up out of the ocean, dragging behind them the limp carcass of a Giant Octopus."

[recording fades, occasional crackles for the remaining 11:02:20]

Artifact 5

Recording marked "TV News One Florida WESH" "July 1, 2012"

Transcript:

"Last spring, an elderly woman named Marlene Spatafora was found with her tongue and lips cut out and her tongue replaced with a strange crustacean. Police blamed her husband, a commercial fisherman, for the cruel murder, but neighbors said that seemed impossible and most of them believe the murder remains unsolved.

"Earlier this month workers at several fisheries started having strange boils and lesions on their hands. Yesterday, one worker's hand fell off and his wife videoed it and put it on youtube. Soon after that, the husband died, and a strange lobster-tail-like crustacean had replaced his tongue. Now citizens are beginning to ask questions.

"Today, the Mayor delivered a statement, saying, 'We all know that during warmer weather bacteria levels can rise, some people get digestive problems, sometimes rashes, that's been going on for years now, it looks like it's just a bad year, but let's not start telling scary stories, cuz that won't serve us, that won't serve our town. If you have sensitivities, just follow special precautions and you can go in the water today. Have a Happy Fourth of July.'"

Artifact 6

Written article, source and author unknown
Marked: "August 3, 2011"

Sea lice, a type of crustacean that is easily incubated by captive fish on farms, have become a significant problem and have been blamed for declining numbers of wild pink salmon, as well as the species that eat them (bears, eagles, orcas and others).

Sea lice are the scourge of salmon farms, they fasten themselves to the caged fish, live off their mucus coating, adversely affecting both the health and appearance of the salmon. In attempts to kill off the parasite, aquaculture operators have developed ways to treat affected fish with pesticides that critics say are harmful to the marine environment in general and to lobsters in particular.

Lobsters, like sea lice, are crustaceans and have the same vulnerabilities to the pesticides that the sea lice do, according to lobster industry officials. If the pesticides are not applied properly, environmentalists and lobster industry officials have said, the chemicals could kill lobsters that are near the pens where salmon are being treated.

Traces of cypermethrin, a pesticide approved in Maine for combating sea lice but banned in Canada, was found in early 2010 in a huge washup of dead lobsters on Deer Island, within a few miles of the American border. According to the Bangor Daily News, the agency Environment Canada is investigating the mysterious lobster deaths.

www.ingramcontent.com/pod-product-compliance
Lightning Source LLC
Chambersburg PA
CBHW021939170626
46807CB00007B/3184